Tales

for the

Perfect Child

FLORENCE PARRY HEIDE

ILLUSTRATED BY SERGIO RUZZIER

Atheneum

ATHENEUM BOOKS FOR YOUNG READERS
NEW YORK   LONDON   TORONTO   SYDNEY   NEW DELHI

Tales

for the

Perfect Child

ALSO BY

FLORENCE PARRY HEIDE
WITH SYLVIA WORTH VAN CLIEF

Fables You Shouldn't Pay Any Attention To

Tales
for the
Perfect Child

ATHENEUM BOOKS FOR YOUNG READERS
An imprint of Simon & Schuster Children's Publishing Division
1230 Avenue of the Americas, New York, New York 10020

ATHENEUM BOOKS FOR YOUNG READERS is a registered
trademark of Simon & Schuster, Inc. Atheneum logo is a trademark
of Simon & Schuster, Inc.
For information about special discounts for bulk purchases,
please contact Simon & Schuster Special Sales at 1-866-506-1949 or
business@simonandschuster.com.
The Simon & Schuster Speakers Bureau can bring authors to your live
event. For more information or to book an event, contact the
Simon & Schuster Speakers Bureau at 1-866-248-3049 or visit our website
at www.simonspeakers.com.
Also available in an Atheneum Books for Young Readers hardcover edition
Book design by Debra Sfetsios-Conover
The text for this book was set in Sabon LT Std.
The illustrations for this book were rendered in pen & ink and ink wash
on paper.
Manufactured in the United States of America
0218 MTN
First Atheneum Books for Young Readers paperback edition March 2018
10 9 8 7 6 5 4 3 2 1

The Library of Congress has cataloged the hardcover edition as follows:
Names: Heide, Florence Parry. | Ruzzier, Sergio, 1966- illustrator.
Title: Tales for the perfect child / Florence Parry Heide ; illustrated by
Sergio Ruzzier.
Description: New York : Atheneum Books for Young Readers, [2017] |
?1985 | Originally published in a different form by Lothrop, Lee & Shepard
Books in 1985. | Summary: Vignettes of children whose less than desirable
behavior is masked in insidious but acceptable ways.
Identifiers: LCCN 2015024594
ISBN 978-1-4814-6379-9 (hc)
ISBN 978-1-4814-6380-5 (pbk)
ISBN 978-1-4814-6381-2 (eBook)

These tales are dedicated
to perfect children, everywhere
—F. P. H.

And also to children
with some imperfections
—S. R.

CONTENTS

Ruby

RUBY WANTED TO GO OVER
to Ethel's house to play. But Ruby's
mother said, "You have to watch
Clyde."

Clyde was Ruby's baby brother.

He had just learned to walk.

"I don't want to watch Clyde. I want to go over to Ethel's house to play," said Ruby.

Ruby's mother was tired. She had been watching Clyde all day. "You have to watch Clyde because I have to take a bubble bath," said Ruby's mother. She went into the bathroom.

Ruby called Ethel. "I'll be over in a minute."

Then Ruby watched Clyde.

She watched him take all of the clothes out of all of the drawers in all of the bureaus in all of the rooms.

She watched him take all of the rice and all of the flour and all of the salt and all of the sugar and all of the coffee out of all of the kitchen cupboards and spill it all on the nice clean floor.

She watched him pull the table-cloth off the kitchen table. The bananas that had been on the table landed on Clyde's head.

Ruby watched Clyde start to cry very loud.

Her mother came out of the bathroom. "What's going on?" she asked. "I told you to watch Clyde."

"I was watching him," said Ruby truthfully. "I was watching him the whole time."

In a few minutes Ruby was ringing Ethel's doorbell. "I told you I'd be over in a minute," she said. "I just had to watch Clyde."

Arthur

ARTHUR LIKED TO WEAR HIS
old comfortable clothes and his old
comfortable sneakers. He did not
like to get dressed up. He did not
like to wear white shirts and nice suits,

13

and he did not like to wear any of the nice ties he had gotten for his birthday.

"Arthur," said his mother, "we're going to visit Aunt Eunice. Put on your white shirt and your nice suit and your new tie and your nice new shiny shoes."

Arthur did not want to get dressed up. He did not want to visit Aunt Eunice. He wanted to stay home in his old clothes and watch his favorite program.

"I want to stay here in my old clothes and watch my favorite program," said Arthur.

"Well, you're going with me to see Aunt Eunice, and that's that. And you're going to get dressed up, and that's that."

Arthur's mother always wanted to tell Arthur what was what. That was very thoughtful. Mothers are thoughtful people.

"All right," said Arthur.

Arthur's mother was surprised. Usually Arthur argued. Arthur was very good at arguing.

Arthur put on his white shirt and his nice new suit and the tie that Aunt Eunice had given him for his last birthday. He put on the new shiny shoes.

"Now you look like a gentle-man," said his mother.

And he did. He looked like a little gentleman.

As soon as he was all dressed up, Arthur went out to the kitchen. He opened the refrigerator. He poured himself a nice big glass of grape juice. Some of it got on his face, but most of it got on his white shirt and the pretty new suit and the tie that Aunt Eunice had given him for his birthday.

Then he went out to the yard.
In a few minutes his nice shiny
shoes were all muddy.

His mother was sad.

"Oh, dear," she said. "You've spoiled all your nice clothes. You can't go to see Aunt Eunice looking like that. You'll have to stay home."

So Arthur changed back into his blue jeans and sweater and his old comfortable sneakers. His mother went to see Aunt Eunice, and Arthur had to stay home and watch his favorite television program.

Gertrude
&
Gloria

CHILDREN SHOULD BE HELPFUL.

That's what Gertrude and Gloria's mother always said. And she was right, just as mothers always are: Children *should* be helpful. They should help with the dishes, for instance. It isn't fair for mothers and fathers to do all the work.

"Help clear the table, dears," said Gertrude and Gloria's mother after dinner.

They started to help.

Gertrude carried the dishes over to the kitchen sink very very carefully.

Gloria was not careful. She

dropped the dishes and broke three

plates. Her mother was not happy.

"Help dry the dishes, dears," said their mother. "And be sure to put them away where they belong." Mothers always like to have everything in the right place. That makes it easier to find things.

Gertrude dried the dishes very

very carefully and put them just where they belonged.

Gloria put the cups where the plates should be, and the plates where the pans should be, and she broke her mother's very best teacup.

Her mother was sad.

She said she would not let Gloria help with the dishes any more.

Since Gertrude had been so extremely careful and helpful, and had done such a very good job, she got to help with the dishes the next day and every day after that.

Good for Gertrude.

Harry

H ARRY DID NOT LIKE CARROTS.

"They're yucky," he said.

"Nonsense," said his mother. She

was a no-nonsense kind of mother.

"Carrots are good for you."

And she was right. Carrots are very good for you.

"They're yucky," said Harry.

And that was true. Carrots *are* yucky if you don't like them.

"Well, you can't have any ice cream until your carrots are gone," said Harry's mother.

Harry pushed his carrots around on his plate. That did not make the carrots go away. And that's what Harry wanted. He

wanted the carrots to go away.

"Eat your carrots, Harry," said Harry's mother. "You won't ever get to like carrots if you don't eat them."

Harry's mother was very wise. You could tell that from the wise things she said.

When she went out to the kitchen, Harry put all of the carrots in a small plastic bag he kept in his pocket for special times.

Then he put the plastic bag back in
his pocket.

Harry's mother came back into
the dining room and saw his empty

plate. "See?" she said. "I told you
you'd like carrots if you tried."

Harry started to eat his ice

cream. *There is always a way to get out of eating something yucky,* he thought.

Bertha

IT WAS A LOVELY, COOL, SUN-

shiny day.

"It's a lovely, cool, sunshiny day,"

said Bertha's mother. "Stop watching

television and go outside and play."

48

Bertha did not want to go outside and play. She wanted to stay indoors and watch cartoons.

"Out you go," said Bertha's mother. "And don't argue."

Bertha wasn't going to try to argue anyway, because Bertha never won arguments with her mother. Mothers usually win arguments. Mothers are bigger than children.

The cartoon was at a very exciting part.

"I'll go outside as soon as I get dressed," said Bertha.

"Well, hurry up," said Bertha's mother.

"I am hurrying," said Bertha.

That was not true. Bertha tried to move very very slowly. It always took her an extremely long time to get ready for anything, especially when she was watching television.

"Hurry up, Bertha," said Bertha's mother.

Bertha had tied knots in her shoelaces so that it would take a very long time to untie them. While she untied the knots, she

watched the cartoon.

Bertha put on one shoe. She put the other shoe in a big vase.

"I can't find my shoe," said Bertha.

"Of course you can," said Bertha's mother. "I'll help you find it. It can't have walked off by itself."

What she said was true: Bertha's shoe couldn't have walked off by itself. Bertha's mother had some very sensible sayings.

Bertha's mother looked and looked, but she could not find Bertha's shoe.

"Well, you can wear your old sneakers," she said finally. "Here they

are. Hurry up and put them on."

"I can't find my jacket," said Bertha.

That was because Bertha had put her jacket in a very secret place.

Bertha's mother looked and looked for the jacket. By the time she found it, it had started to rain.

Bertha settled down in front of the television set. It was a lovely, cool, rainy day.

Harriet

HARRIET WAS A VERY GOOD
whiner. She practiced and practiced, and so of course she got better and better at it. Practice makes
perfect.

Some children hardly ever whine. Can you believe that? So of course they never get to be very good at it.

"Can I have a piece of that blueberry pie?" Harriet asked her mother while her mother was fixing dinner.

Guests were coming, and her mother wanted everything to be very nice.

"No, Harriet. The pie is for

after dinner. We're having roast
beef."

Children like Harriet are not

interested in roast beef when they are interested in pie.

"I want a piece of pie," whined Harriet. She used her best whiny voice.

"I said no and I mean no," said Harriet's mother. She always liked to say what she meant.

Harriet's mother started to make some nice tomato aspic.

Harriet kept whining, "Can I have some pie, can I have some pie?"

Harriet's mother kept saying that when she said no she meant no. Harriet's mother tried to concentrate on the aspic, but that was very hard to do because Harriet was whining.

Good whiners make it very

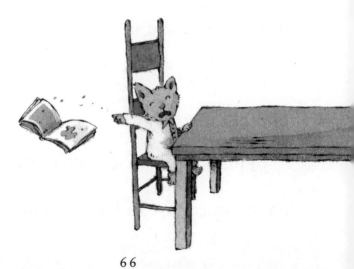

hard for anyone to think of anything else.

"Why don't you color in your
nice new coloring book?" asked
Harriet's mother.

"I want some pie now," whined
Harriet.

"Dinner will be ready pretty soon," said Harriet's mother.

"But I want some pie *now*," whined Harriet.

A good whiner sticks to one subject. A good whiner never gives up.

Harriet kept whining, and her mother kept trying to get dinner ready.

"I want some pie," whined Harriet, and her mother burned the gravy.

"All right, all right," her mother

said. She was very tired of hearing

Harriet whine.

Harriet stopped whining while she had her piece of pie. She always rested up between whines. That's what good whiners always do.

Irving

IRVING WAS VISITING HIS
cousin Irma.

Irving did not like to visit Irma.
The reason Irving did not like to
visit Irma was because Irving did

not like Irma. The reason Irving
did not like Irma was because Irma
always got her own way. The reason Irma always got her own way
was because Irma's parents did not
like Irma to cry and carry on. And

Irma always cried and carried on when she didn't get her own way.

This Saturday afternoon, Irma's parents were planning to take Irma and Irving to a lovely piano recital at Miss Meesley's house.

Irma was the kind of person who liked piano recitals and concerts and educational programs. Irving was the kind of person who liked baseball and circuses and movies.

Before they left for the recital at Miss Meesley's house, Irving said to Irma, "It's too bad about the bats at Miss Meesley's."

"Bats?" asked Irma, and her eyes grew unusually large. Usually her eyes were unusually small.

"What bats?" Irma was the kind of person who was very very afraid of bats.

"I suppose your parents didn't want to tell you," said Irving. "Miss Meesley has a problem with bats this week. Swooping bats. They start to swoop when they hear the music." Irving never cared whether he told a lie or not.

"Besides, there's a very good movie," said Irving. "There are no bats in the theater," he added.

"Okay," said Irma. "We'll go to the movie instead."

Irma's parents did not want to
go to the movie instead, but Irma
cried and carried on, and so she
got her own way.

They all went to the movie

instead of the lovely piano recital.

Irving decided he probably liked

Irma better than he'd thought.

Ethel

Emma was kind.

Rose was helpful.

Gladys was very polite.

Ernest was the kind of person
who *shared*.

And Ethel was a perfect child.
You don't meet many of those.

But then something terrible happened. Ethel discovered bubble gum. Isn't that awful?

Of course Ethel's mother and father hated bubble gum. All parents hate bubble gum, and parents know best.

They didn't like the way Ethel

chewed it, they didn't like the way

Ethel popped it, they didn't like the way Ethel blew great big beautiful bubbles with it, and they didn't like the way it stuck to everything.

"We don't ever want to see you chewing bubble gum again, Ethel," her parents told her.

And they never did.

That doesn't mean that Ethel stopped chewing bubble gum. Oh, no. But her parents never *saw* her chewing it.

That's another good thing about Ethel. Ethel was a very sensible person.

The End

FLORENCE PARRY HEIDE (1919–2011) was the author of more than one hundred children's books, including picture books, juvenile novels, two series of young-adult mysteries, plays, songbooks, and poetry. She may be best remembered for her now-classic *The Shrinking of Treehorn* and its two sequels, illustrated by the great Edward Gorey. Florence grew up in Punxsutawney, Pennsylvania, married during the Second World War, and spent her adult life in Kenosha, Wisconsin, with her husband and five children, all of whom grew up listening to the joyful sounds of an old typewriter.

SERGIO RUZZIER has written and illustrated many picture books. He was awarded the Sendak Fellowship in 2011. Born in Italy, he lives in Brooklyn, New York. Visit Sergio online at Ruzzier.com.